LIVING STORIES ABOUT LIV.

Connected Wisdom

by Linda Booth Sweeney, Ed.D.

SEED

ABOUT SEED

Since 1998, Schlumberger Excellence in Educational Development (SEED) has been connecting scientists, teachers, and students around the world to ignite a passion for science and learning. With the support of Schlumberger volunteers, teachers and students at SEED network schools participate in intensive, hands-on projects. Many of these projects explore the complexity of living systems and how they relate to global themes such as water, climate change, and energy. The SEED Web site and online Science Center host a growing library of tools and articles that enlighten learners about the water cycle, the carbon cycle, sustainable energy sources, and global climate change—a wealth of knowledge that relates to the systems-based views presented by Connected Wisdom. To learn more about SEED, visit www.seed.slb.com.

ABOUT THE AUTHOR

Linda Booth Sweeney, Ed.D., is a systems educator, researcher, and writer, who is dedicated to helping people of all ages learn to embed everyday decisions with a deeper understanding of living systems principles. She works with SEED and Schlumberger to integrate the principles and tools of systems thinking into the SEED educational materials including the SEED web site. Linda lectures widely, translating the conceptual ideas of systems theory into programs, tools, and materials for educational and organizational transformation. Her particular passion is helping young people discover their own natural systems intelligence through innovative books and articles, web site content, puppet shows, museum displays, and computer simulations. Linda is the author of several books, including *The Systems Thinking Playbook* (currently translated into Chinese and Russian) and *When a Butterfly Sneezes: A Guide for Helping Children Explore Interconnections in Our World through Favorite Stories*. She has contributed to numerous magazines and academic journals.

ACKNOWLEDGEMENTS

My heartfelt thanks to Simone Amber of SEED, who early on, saw how theses folktales could contribute to SEED's rich library of science literacy resources and activities. I am grateful for Milton Glaser's world-class art direction, to Molly Kromhout for her graceful, expert graphic design, and to Guy Billout for his beautiful, enigmatic illustrations. To the team at SEED—Love Zubiller, Michael Tempel, Susan Randel, and Eya Tkachenko—thank you for making it possible for SEED students, teachers, and volunteers around the world to enjoy this book.

As an educator, I am grateful to those "scientists"—Peter Senge, Fritjof Capra, and Mary Catherine Bateson—who over the years have patiently answered my questions and who generously read early drafts of this book. I am also grateful to my amazing circle of colleagues and friends, all of whom greatly enhanced this book through their careful readings and commentary.

I am indebted to Margaret Read MacDonald for her generous help in identifying relevant folktales and to the deft editorial assistance of Karen Speerstra, Jennifer Margulis, and Gale Pryor. I am especially thankful to my parents, Bob and Rosemarie Booth, and my husband, John, who enthusiastically read every draft I put in front of them. And finally, I'd like to thank my children, Jack, Ted, and Anna Rose for listening to me read literally hundreds of folktales and helping me find "just the right one."

Published internationally by SEED (Schlumberger Excellence in Educational Development)

© 2008 Schlumberger and Linda Booth Sweeney. All rights reserved.

Author: Linda Booth Sweeney

Design: Milton Glaser, Inc.

Illustration: Guy Billout

Printer: Regent Publishing Services, Ltd.

Printed in China.

TABLE OF CONTENTS

Introduction   1

Chapter 1 *Interdependence*   7

Chapter 2 *Systems Integrity*   15

Chapter 3 *Biodiversity*   20

Chapter 4 *Cooperation and Partnership*   29

Chapter 5 *Rightness of Size*   35

Chapter 6 *The Commons*   41

Chapter 7 *Living Cycles*   46

Chapter 8 *Waste = Food*   52

Chapter 9 *Balancing Feedback*   61

Chapter 10 *Reinforcing Feedback*   67

Chapter 11 *Nonlinearity*   72

Chapter 12 *Earth Time*   79

Appendix A   85

Appendix B   91

Note: Additional content is published online at www.seed.slb.com

INTRODUCTION

In a spider's web, what happens on one part of the web affects every other part. The same is true of a living system, whether it be an ant colony, a forest, or a city. Like a spider's web, a living system is so intricately woven that no part exists in isolation. Like a web, a living system is both purposeful and beautiful. With the wisdom of ancient storytellers, this book celebrates living systems, how they affect us and are affected by us.

On a field trip to Walden Pond in Concord, Massachusetts, a group of nine-year-olds gathers to sit quietly and draw nature, just as the 19th century American naturalist and philosopher Henry David Thoreau did, in the same spot, more than 150 years earlier. As class chaperone, I watch as a debate erupts about what is and isn't "nature."

"I can't draw you," a boy named Tom says to a classmate. "You're not part of nature."

"Yeah" another student pipes in, "people *use* nature. We aren't nature."

Another classmate named Christina, sitting on the ground against a tree trunk, disagrees: "No way, you guys, we *are* nature! So you can draw this tree and you can draw me, too."

Who is right?

In a sense, they both are because everyone is entitled to have an opinion. From Christina's perspective, there's no separation between humans and nature. In Tom's view, if we exist outside of nature, we're free to take from it to meet our needs without consequences. Yet when we see ourselves as separate from nature, we tend to create problems that can be hard to fix, such as polluted water, animal extinction, and global warming.

If we think like Tom, we forget that nature can teach us a lot. We may even forget that just as with the laws we follow in our own countries, there are also laws of nature we follow. Think of it like this: In most countries the law says vehicles must stop at red traffic lights. It's the law. Littering is illegal in most countries. Wherever we go, we must learn and follow the laws. We all follow other laws—natural laws. Throw an apple from a window and what happens? It falls to the ground. Not one of us expects the apple to fall up. Gravity is just one of nature's laws. Others may not be as well known but are just as fascinating and just as certain.

If we understand nature's laws, we can work with them, rather than disrupt them. In nature, for instance, there is no such thing as waste. One species' waste is another's food; everybody is somebody's lunch. If we, as fellow inhabitants of this Earth, follow and learn from nature's laws, we too can live sustainably, or within the means of nature on this planet.

In this book, we explore 12 of those natural laws (or principles):

1. INTERDEPENDENCE
2. SYSTEMS INTEGRITY
3. BIODIVERSITY
4. COOPERATION AND PARTNERSHIP
5. RIGHTNESS OF SIZE
6. THE COMMONS
7. LIVING CYCLES
8. WASTE = FOOD
9. BALANCING FEEDBACK
10. REINFORCING FEEDBACK
11. NONLINEARITY
12. EARTH TIME

Nature, of course, isn't governed by these 12 laws alone. There are many more, including: the first and second laws of thermodynamics, carrying capacity, exponential growth, and nested systems among others (for more about these laws, see Appendix A).

LIVING SYSTEMS

Like Tom, Christina, and the other students at Walden Pond that day, we can learn about these laws by simply observing nature. When we study nature we begin to see patterns, ways in which nature tends to behave. But what makes nature a vast living system?

We use the phrase *living systems* as a metaphor, to represent an animate arrangement of parts and processes that continually affect one another other over time. There are living systems on all scales, from the smallest plankton to the human body to the planet as a whole. When we understand what makes up a living system, we can see that a family, a business, and even a country also are living systems.

One way to identify a living system is by observing if it changes over time. Mechanical systems, such as a car or a computer, do not grow or evolve. They are built in a certain way and stay that way until someone replaces a part. On the other hand, living systems grow.

Another way is to observe how the parts of a system are connected. Most mechanical systems, such as a telephone or a tractor, are built to work—and be fixed—in straightforward ways. When a machine stops working, there's usually a trained expert such as a mechanic, a plumber, or a computer whiz who can find the cause and fix the problem. There is usually a straight line between a problem and its solution.

Living systems, on the other hand, are rarely made up of straight lines. Instead they're composed of patterns of connection and interaction that better resemble loops, webs, and networks. Although we can't see these patterns, we know they're capable of producing breathtaking synergy in nature and present some of the most puzzling and stubborn challenges we face as humans.

When a problem occurs in a living system, there may not be a straight line to the solution, because the ever-changing connections curve and loop, building on some changes and canceling out others. In the living system of a school, homework is good, yet too much of it can lead to a downward spiral of student fatigue, loss of motivation, and poor grades. In the living system of a farm, spraying pesticides to control bothersome pests can sometimes create bigger problems. The pesticides can also wipe out the insects that ate the pests that ate the plants. And in the living system of a city, building a highway to solve traffic congestion can often result in more drivers on the road and in the end, more traffic congestion.

While we can easily observe the individual parts of a living system—for instance, the animals in a rain forest or the departments in an organization—it is often difficult to see the whole system. The connections between the parts are an important aspect of the living system. To see most systems, and to understand how they function, we have to visualize the connections that make up a whole system.

As we begin to see the interconnections, rather than the parts, and to understand how they bend and weave and change over time, our view of the world begins to change. When we look at the ocean, we see not just the surface of the water but also the plankton, kelp forest, mollusks, fish, sharks, whales, and seabirds that feed on one another. We see the fishing fleets, fish markets, and families eating seafood. We see trash and other pollution going into the sea. We see all the world's parts in a continually changing web of interrelationships. We see that nothing exists in isolation.

THE WISDOM OF FOLKTALES

There are many ways to learn about living systems. People at universities around the world study the science of these systems. Popular books describe the systems for every reader. But another way to learn about living systems—and change our view of the world—is by listening to stories that have been told for centuries.

One night I was reading *Aesop's Fables* with my son Jack. We were flipping through the book, looking for "The Boy Who Cried Wolf," when Jack stopped at the story "Hercules and Pallas." "Oh!" he said, looking at the picture of Hercules whacking a fierce-looking monster called Strife. "Let's read that one!"

In the story, Hercules and Strife are locked in a mounting battle of wills. With every whack from Hercules, Strife grows bigger. Only when Hercules stops attacking Strife does Strife start to diminish in size. When we finished the story, I asked Jack if this tale sounded familiar to him. "Have you seen this happen in real life?" I asked. He nodded and pointed to his four-year-old brother, asleep on the sofa. He explained how sometimes when he teased his little brother, his brother poked him back. Then one poke led to a bigger poke and then to tears.

Jack had picked up on a living system law or principle—called reinforcing feedback—illustrated by the story. Reinforcing feedback occurs when a change builds on itself over time. In the language of living systems, this particular kind of reinforcing feedback is often called *escalation*. In escalation, one party does something that is seen as a threat by another party, so the other party responds in kind, increasing the threat to the first party. This results in even more threatening actions by the first party, and so the spiral continues. Competing street gangs, the advertising campaigns of rival soft drinks, and the Israeli-Palestinian conflict all share a similar pattern of escalation.

After we read the story, I asked Jack what he might do differently with his little brother. He thought for a moment and said, "Maybe it's better if I just leave him alone."

What happened? For one precious moment, Jack experienced a subtle but powerful shift in understanding. When Jack saw himself as part of, rather than separate from, a living system (the system of siblings), it changed his view of "the problem." He saw the connection between his actions and the actions of another. And now, when I see that pattern of sibling rivalry starting, I can say: "Remember that story about Hercules and Strife?"

I believe the Greek philosopher Aristotle had it right when he said, "The friend of wisdom is also a friend of myth." Folk wisdom—whether it comes from the myths and tales of the ancient Greeks, the Africans, the fifth-century Chinese philosophers, the Buddhist masters, or the sages of Native American and other cultures—has long been a way to pass on wisdom from one generation to the next. Many folktales and myths, such as those in this book, were used by the ancients to explain and understand the physical world around us. Today, as we learn to live sustainably on this planet, one of our challenges is to remember what we already know. The stories of the ancients can help us to do that.

In my own journey to make living systems more accessible to children and adults, I found myself apprenticed to a humble Greek slave named Aesop, who over two thousand years ago created clever tales to entertain nobles in the court of the powerful King Croesus.

One teacher wasn't enough, however, so I sit as a student to many other masters, including the Sufis of a thousand years ago, centuries-old Ashanti tale tellers from West Africa, Turkish storytellers from five centuries ago, the Brothers Grimm and other Germans from the early 1800s, the American folklorists of the nineteenth century, and Native American, Brazilian, Japanese, Chinese, Maori, Irish fabulists and a wealth of fabulists from many other cultures that span the ages. I've also learned from the professional storytellers and academics of today, for example Margaret Read MacDonald, who has studied world folktales and myths and organized them by motif and themes, such as the trickster tales found in the folklore of numerous peoples.

This book is for students, educators, parents, and anyone who wants to make everyday decisions within the context of an understanding of living systems principles. In it, I've gathered the wisdom of those who have come before us to share their stories and principles by adapting many of the folktales for my readers.

I hope you find pleasure in the stories you find within these pages. Share them generously, and may your apprenticeship in living systems be enjoyable and fruitful.

Linda Booth Sweeney

CONCORD, MASSACHUSETTS
JULY 30, 2008

CHAPTER

INTERDEPENDENCE

A RELATIONSHIP IN WHICH EACH PARTNER AFFECTS
AND OFTEN NEEDS THE OTHER

What does a corn harvest in Iowa have to do with a little boy on the African savanna? What does a wolf have to do with an aspen tree? Or the tree outside your window with the breath you're about to take?

One thing connects to another, and another, and another. Sometimes the connections are clear; sometimes they aren't. But if we open our eyes to how all things interact and how those interactions change other things—which then interact—we begin to see the world differently. We begin to focus on interconnectedness—of species, people, oceans, even of countries—rather than on separate elements.

Leonardo da Vinci, the great genius of the Italian Renaissance, might have used the word *connessione* ("connection") for this

way of seeing the world: yet, Leonardo was not the first person to recognize and appreciate how everything in the world connects. People across the Earth and throughout time have told one another about interdependence in their stories. They've warned of the *problems* of unintended consequences, when a solution to one problem actually leads to a bigger problem, which leads to a growing spiral of solutions and problems. They've also told about the *opportunities* of interdependence, when interactions create something that is more than the sum of its parts, such as teamwork, healthy ecosystems, and thriving communities.

In this Balinese folktale, Gecko discovers he is connected to all the other members of his jungle community in ways he never knew.

Gecko's Complaint

One night a Village Chief was awakened out of a deep sleep by five calls of "Geck-o, Geck-o, Geck-o, Geck-o, Geck-o." It was Gecko the lizard. "I must see the chief. I'm not happy!"

Being a wise and kindly man, the Chief received him even though it was in the middle of the night.

To the rest of his fellow creatures, it might have seemed that Gecko had no reason at all to complain. He could do so many things that other creatures could not do. With the pads on the tip of his toes, he could walk up a wall or hang upside down from the ceiling. And he could grow a new tail if he lost one in battle. No other animal could do that.

"Gecko, what do you have to complain about?" the Chief asked.

"I can't sleep. Night after night, Firefly bothers me with his sparks of fire."

"I have heard you. I will speak to Firefly," the Chief told Gecko. "Now go back to your house and try to sleep."

The next day the Chief called Firefly and told him about Gecko's complaint. "Is it only Gecko you are disturbing?" he asked. "Or is it possible that others are also bothered by your light flashing into their eyes?"

It was daytime, so Firefly's light was no longer burning, and he spoke very humbly to the Chief. "I meant no harm, Sir. In fact, I thought I was doing something good. I heard the drumming of Woodpecker as he struck his bill on the tree trunk, and I thought it was a *kulkul* drum calling the villagers to awake and gather together. I was only flashing my light to pass on the message."

The Chief then decided to ask Woodpecker about this. He found him, boring away with his chisel-like bill, and told him what Firefly had said.

"I, too, was only sounding an alarm, Sir," said Woodpecker. "I heard the *kwak-kwak-kwak* of Frog in the rice paddies, and I thought it was a warning that an earthquake was coming. So I just passed on the message."

The Chief went in search of Frog, who, meanwhile, had heard that he would be interrogated. Even before the Chief could ask, he said: "The reason I was *kwak-kwak-kwaking* more and louder than usual is that I saw Black Beetle walking down the road carrying muck, which I thought was so dirty and so unhealthy that I had to stop him."

That is indeed bad, thought the Chief. I must speak to Beetle at once.

Black Beetle, plump and gleaming like polished copper, was also very humble and respectful as he explained the situation to the Chief.

"You see, Sir, Water Buffalo comes by so often dropping his pat in the middle of the road that I just thought it was my duty to clean it up."

The Chief was now beginning to lose his patience. "Tell Water Buffalo I wish to see him at once!" he ordered.

Then Water Buffalo slowly approached. He, too, was polite, but he expressed great displeasure with Black Beetle's report. "It's clear," he said, "that I'm not appreciated. Rain washes away all the stones in the road, and I fill up the holes. Who else does that, I ask you?"

The Village Chief was getting very tired, but he decided that he had better listen to Rain's story next. When he found Rain, he realized Rain was very angry.

"Water Buffalo was complaining about ME?" he asked. Without ME, there are no mosquitoes, and if there are no mosquitoes, Gecko is hungry and unhappy. Don't speak to me. Speak to Gecko!"

So the Chief called Gecko in once more. In a stern voice he said, "Gecko, no more complaining! We're all connected in ways we sometimes can't see. Go home, and live at peace with all your neighbors."

And so Gecko did.

How often do we find ourselves like Gecko, annoyed by things others do or frustrated by events when we don't understand the reason they occur? Also like Gecko, we may find that the source of our problems becomes clear—and may even go away—when we shift our focus from protecting our independence to understanding our interdependence.

American civil rights activist the Reverend Dr. Martin Luther King Jr. came to a similar conclusion in a 1967 sermon: "It really boils down to this: that all life is interrelated. We are all caught in an inescapable network of mutuality, tied into a single garment of destiny. Whatever affects one directly, affects all indirectly … We aren't going to have peace on Earth until we recognize this basic fact of the interrelated structure of all reality."

Interdependence: A relationship of interlocking needs that contain elements of both difference and commonality.

CHAPTER

SYSTEMS INTEGRITY

WHAT A SYSTEM HAS WHEN ALL THE PARTS AND PROCESSES ESSENTIAL
TO ITS ABILITY TO FUNCTION ARE PRESENT

I magine that you get on a bus and take your seat. You're ready to leave, when all of a sudden the driver unscrews the steering wheel and throws it out the door. Then a passenger walks up and removes the brake pedal and throws it out the window. You look outside and see a mechanic opening up the hood and removing the engine! Before you can say anything, the bus starts moving. What's going on? You can't remove parts from a mechanical system and expect it to work, right?

Yet we do it all the time with living systems. We tinker with elements in the natural world and expect it to continue working all the same. In the 1920s, for instance, ranchers, angered that wolves were attacking some of their sheep and cattle, called for all wolves to be removed from Yellowstone National Park in the

western United States. Over the next 70 years, wildlife biologists and park rangers watched as the integrity, or the "wholeness," of the Yellowstone ecosystem fell apart. Without the wolves, moose and elk herds grew unchecked. Free to roam, the herds overgrazed shrubs and plants, which meant fewer nesting areas for migrating birds, changing habitats for beaver colonies, and so on. The wolves were returned to Yellowstone in 1995. This has helped to restore the park's health and integrity.

Animal habitats, your family, your school, and the global economy are all systems with integrity. Think about the human body. Our bodies are much more than just sacks of unconnected organs. Each is a living system, with integrity. If something happens to an essential part, such as the heart, or to a process, such as the transformation of food into energy, the body won't feel well or may not function at all.

Here's another way to think about systems integrity: What do you get if you cut a cow in half? Most children know that you don't get two cows. Ask any child this question, and she will tell you that the parts of the cow "belong together" or that "they need each other" to live. All the parts and processes necessary for the cow to function and live are present. The cow, as a system, has integrity.

When we pay attention to a system's integrity, as we make decisions we continually ask: What will happen to the whole if a part or a process is removed?

In this folktale from the Philippines, when the parts of the house argue about which is most important, integrity is lost and disharmony creeps in.

The Parts of the House Argue

A large family once lived together in a palm tree house. One day the people in the house began to quarrel about which was the most important member of the family. Before long, even the parts of the house began to quarrel.

The poles that supported the house high off the ground started grumbling. One said, "I am the most important because I was driven into the Earth first." Feeling very quarrelsome, the rest of the poles replied, "We're all just as important as you, because without us you couldn't do your job of keeping the house off the wet ground!"

Just then, the floor supports began to shout, "No one would care about the poles if we weren't here to connect you!"

That made the cross supports under the floor cry out: "Without us, you'd wobble and sag!"

The floor snapped back to the cross supports and the floor supports: "Without me, neither of you would have a reason to exist."

It was then that the four woven bamboo walls chimed in, rather nastily, down to the floor, "Who would walk on you if we weren't here to create rooms?"

In anger, the roof beams replied to the walls, "You couldn't stand up if it were not for our support!"

Then the bamboo ceiling shouted to the beams, "I hold the walls together!"

And, finally, the palm-leaf roof joined in by chiding each

part of the house, "I keep the rain from rotting all of you!"

As they argued, they realized that none could win the argument since they were all of great use to the house. So they each took a big breath and together proclaimed, "None is important without the other." As soon as the house stopped quarreling, so did the family. Cured of misfortune, the family lived in peace and harmony from that day forward. And the house is still standing.

When the parts of the house finally realize that "none is important without the other," they know they, and the house as a whole, cannot function without one another. Just like the parts of the house, we, too, can become blind to the contribution of all the elements that give integrity to the systems around us. And when integrity is lost, we feel a sense of disharmony and imbalance.

Systems Integrity: What a system has when all the parts and processes essential to its ability to function are present.

CHAPTER

BIODIVERSITY

THE VARIETY, COMPLEXITY, AND ABUNDANCE OF SPECIES THAT, IF
ADEQUATE, MAKE ECOSYSTEMS HEALTHY AND RESILIENT

Close your eyes and imagine yourself in a magnificent pine forest. Stand still. Listen. What do you hear? One bird calls, "Chick-a-dee-dee-dee-dee." Other chickadees answer. What do you see? Ferns, fungi, mosses, wildflowers, vines, shrubs, insects, birds, and many small animals. The scent of the pines welcomes you. You might catch glimpses of bears, beavers, and deer. All around you are living creatures in a riot of colors and sounds and smells.

Ecologists can gauge the health of an ecosystem by how many different kinds of inhabitants it holds. The greater the diversity of species, the healthier, the more resilient, and the more flexible the ecosystem. Conservationists work to preserve the biodiversity of wilderness regions around the world. What about the

biodiversity of areas in which we live and work? Maintaining open space, or areas that do not have buildings or roads; "critter crossings" (tunnels or bridges that allow wildlife to safely cross highways and busy roads); and gardens are all ways to support biodiversity, even in cities and suburbs.

When we conserve the diversity of species in all environments, we help ourselves as well as other species. Maintaining marshlands and mangrove forests in coastal areas, for instance, protects coastal communities against major storms as well as supporting local plant and animal species. When the population of several species of vultures from India and South Asia plummeted, scientists discovered that they were being killed by a drug commonly given to cattle. The vultures fed on cattle carcasses in the area and were poisoned by the drug. Without the vultures to eat them, the dead animals festered in the hot sun. Wild dogs, freed of competition with the vultures, gorged on the cows. With more food, the wild dog population exploded, greatly increasing the threat of the disease rabies. Saving the vultures and preserving the biodiversity of the region became essential to protecting people from a dangerous disease.

When we embrace the living systems principle of biodiversity, we understand the importance of, as 20th century American conservationist Aldo Leopold once wrote, keeping "every cog and wheel" and saving as many species as possible. In doing so, we also enrich and protect our own lives.

In this folktale from Sierra Leone, a kingdom's seemingly unremarkable subjects surprise even the wisest chief and teach him an important lesson about diversity.

Kanu Above and Kanu Below

Kanu Above and Kanu Below were both great chiefs. Kanu Above lived in the skies. Kanu Below lived on the Earth with his beautiful daughter. He loved her very much. But one day Kanu Above said, "I want her to come and live with me." So Kanu Above took her up to Sky Country, while Kanu Below sat alone. He wept for his missing daughter and began to neglect his chiefly duties.

One day his under-chief came to Kanu Below and said, "I must speak with you. Someone has come into our village who is making trouble. His name is Spider, and he is weaving sticky webs over everyone's doorways. People are tripping and hurting themselves. What shall we do?"

Kanu Below said, "Send Spider to me." Spider came and listened as Kanu Below explained why he should not spin harmful webs across people's doorways. Then Kanu Below went back to his people and said, "We will keep Spider among us for a while.

"Yes, he has caused some difficulties, but he also has much good in him."

And it was so.

Two days later, Kanu Below was approached by another under-chief, saying, "Oh, Kanu. Now another stranger has entered our village. His name is Rat, and he is sneaking into our people's houses and stealing rice, meat, and koala nuts."

Again Kanu Below asked that the stranger be brought to him. "Rat, you cannot go into people's houses and take things that

are not yours." And again, Kanu Below spoke to his people, explaining that Rat had done some terrible things but he had much good in him and they would keep him in their village.

And it was so.

Before he knew it, Kanu Below was once more approached by a troubled under-chief.

"Kanu Below, we have yet a third stranger who has entered our village. This time his name is Anteater, and he is digging up everybody's backyards. People are falling into the holes and breaking their legs. This must not go on!"

"Tell Anteater to come to see me." Kanu explained to Anteater that he must not dig holes, because people were falling into them. Then he spoke to his people saying, "I think we should keep Anteater in our village. Yes, he has caused some trouble, but he also has much good in him."

And it was so.

Time passed, and one day the under-chief approached Kanu Below and said, "Kanu, another stranger has entered our village. His name is Fly, and he is biting and stinging people on their necks and on their behinds. Whatever shall we do?"

"Tell Fly to come to see me." Again Kanu explained how his people must not be bitten. Then he said to his chiefs, "It is true that Fly has hurt many people, but he has much good in him as well. I think he should stay in our village."

And it was so.

Many days passed, and Kanu Below was still very sad and spent most of the day weeping for his missing daughter. One day he called his people together and said, "If only someone could climb up into the sky and speak to Kanu Above about my daughter. Perhaps he would listen and return her to me."

Most people were afraid of Kanu Above because he was so powerful. So no one volunteered to go. Then Spider, in a little voice said, "Kanu Below, I will go for you. I will spin a web up, up into the sky." Then other voices joined Spider's and said, "You have treated us well. We would like to help, too."

So it was that Spider spun his web and fastened it onto a cloud. Spider, Rat, Anteater, and Fly climbed it and began walking around Sky Country, calling for Kanu Above. "We come from Kanu Below who misses his daughter very much. Can you please return her to him?"

Kanu Above heard them and approached, glaring at them. "Very well, come and sit down and we shall have some food." He whispered to one of the women, and Fly decided to follow her to the kitchen. When the food was served, Fly buzzed to his friends, "Do not eat the meat! It has been poisoned." So Rat, Anteater, and Spider said, "Thank you, Sir. But we do not eat meat in our country." Instead they politely nibbled from their bowls of rice and palm oil sauce.

Soon it was time to go to bed. They had no sooner entered their sleeping quarters when they heard doors and windows being locked from the outside. Days went by, and they had nothing to eat or drink. Finally, Rat said, "This is a job for me," and began gnawing through the wood. Then he went to various houses and stole rice and nuts and meat and fed his friends.

Kanu's men saw that they were still alive. They brought brush to set fire to the house. Anteater said, "Here is a job for me." Anteater began to dig. Faster and faster he dug. Finally he dug a hole right under the wall. The four friends escaped.

Kanu Above said to himself, *These creatures are very clever!* He explained to them: "I will return the child if you can pick her out from all the other children here." Fly buzzed into the dressing room and noticed one girl who received no help from the others. She had to braid her own hair and put on her own beads, bracelets, and ankle jewelry.

Fly flew back to his friends and cautioned them, "The girls will all be dressed alike, but watch which one jumps. That is our friend's daughter." Fly buzzed over all the girls and, spotting the one he knew to be the "outsider," he bit her. Whoop! She immediately jumped. The four friends grabbed her and said, "This is the one. We choose her."

Kanu Above said, "You are very clever, indeed. Take the girl, and here are four koala nuts for her father, to show my admiration for the four of you."

So the four friends climbed back down with their precious cargo and presented the happy girl to her father, along with the four koala nuts.

"See this," Kanu Below said to his people. "You wanted to banish these four from our village, but it is they who have returned my daughter to me. I am so grateful to them that I have decided they will be my under-chiefs from now on."

And it was so.

In this tale, the sticky-web-building spider, the food-stealing rat, the biting fly, and the hole-digging anteater are considered a nuisance. The wise chief Kanu Below helps the villagers to see that it is the very diversity of these "troublemakers" that makes it possible for them to save his daughter. In much the same way, human communities, like ecological communities, are healthier, more resilient, and more flexible when they have greater diversity.

Biodiversity: the variety, complexity, and abundance of species that, if adequate, make ecosystems healthy and resilient.

CHAPTER

COOPERATION AND PARTNERSHIP

THE CONTINUAL PROCESS IN WHICH SPECIES EXCHANGE ENERGY
AND RESOURCES

While sharing is difficult for most young children, sharing is a way of life for most species of animals. After a kill, for example, wolves leave behind or "share" their leftovers with many others. The animals come to eat in shifts: first, coyotes and foxes pounce on the remains of the wolf hunt. Then bears and large birds such as eagles, crows, ravens, magpies, and vultures come to eat. Woodpeckers, nuthatches, blue jays, and other small birds follow to feast. As night falls, weasels and skunks slink in to pick at the remains, and little rodents scamper about, getting their share of the calcium-rich bones.

Yet the feast isn't over. Invertebrates, parasites, and other organisms, tiny but mighty clean-up crews, help to decompose the leftovers, enriching the soil and encouraging grasses and

other plants to grow. Moose, elk, and deer eat the grass, fattening themselves up for winter and, a few, for the next wolf hunt. Eventually the shared feast begins all over again. In this seemingly predatory world, cooperation prevails.

Indeed, for over three billion years, life on Earth has thrived not through combat or domination but through cooperation and partnership. "The tendency to associate, establish links, live inside one another, and cooperate," writes the physicist Fritjof Capra, "is one of the hallmarks of life." Nature gives of myriad examples of cooperation and partnership among species. The cleaner fish, for example, swims into a shark's mouth and eats left-over food particles from the shark's teeth. It's a perfect partnership: The cleaner fish is well-fed and the shark's teeth are well cleaned.

While companies, cities and nations often emphasize competition and expansion to make their economies grow, we also know that cooperation and partnership are central to creating a sustainable and just world for all. Our challenge lies in reconciling the tensions between competition and cooperation.

In the classic tale of "Stone Soup," (also known as "Axe Soup" and "Nail Soup" in some Scandinavian and European countries), thrifty villagers are awakened to their own lack of cooperation and partnership by a wandering traveler bearing a simple stone.

Stone Soup

A kindly old stranger was walking through the country-side when he came upon a poor village. As he drew near, the villagers entered their homes and locked their doors and windows.

The stranger smiled and asked, "Why are you all so frightened? I am a simple traveler looking for a warm place for a meal and a soft place to sleep for the night."

"There is not a bite to eat in the whole province," he was told. "We are weak, and our children are starving. Better keep moving on."

"Oh, I have everything I need," he said. "In fact, I was thinking of making some stone soup to share with all of you." And he pulled an iron cauldron from his cloak, filled it with water from the village well, and began to build a fire under it.

Then, with great ceremony, he drew an ordinary-looking stone from a silken bag and dropped it into the water.

By now, hearing the rumor of food, most of the villagers slowly came out of their homes, while others watched from their windows. As the stranger sniffed the "broth" and licked his lips in anticipation, hunger began to overcome the villagers' fear.

"Ah," the stranger said to himself rather loudly, "I do like a tasty stone soup. Of course, stone soup with cabbage—now, that's hard to beat."

Soon a villager hesitantly approached, holding a small cab-

bage he had dug from his garden, and added it to the pot.

"Wonderful!" cried the stranger. "You know, I once had stone soup with carrots and a bit of potato as well."

In no time, another villager arrived with a handful of potatoes. Then another with a bunch of carrots.

"A good stone soup should have onions and mushrooms, but why ask for what we don't have?" said the stranger.

"I think I can probably find some onions in my cellar," one woman said. "And I know a place in woods where a few mushrooms may be growing," another said, and off they scurried.

Stirring in the onions and mushrooms, the stranger mused: "With a bit of salt beef, ahh, this would be fit for a king."

"Fit for a king!" the villagers exclaimed. Soon the village butcher showed up with a large hunk of salted beef he had hidden in the back of his shop and added it to the steaming pot. In no time at all, there was a delicious meal for everyone in the village to share.

That night, the kindly old stranger was offered a bed in the mayor's house, the finest house in the village.

As he left the village the next day, the stranger came upon a group of children playing in the field beyond. As he handed a silken bag to the youngest in the group, he said with a smile: "It was not the stone but the people of your village who performed the magic."

The story of "Stone Soup" is as much about cooperation as it is about scarcity. When things become scarce for the villagers, they find themselves acting miserly, thinking only in terms of their own survival. With the help of a humble but clever traveler, they find that renewed strength, and a delicious soup, can come from cooperation, partnership, and generosity. So it is in nature. While there is a role for competition in the evolution of different species, the survival of every life form, from cells on up, depends on cooperation and partnership.

Cooperation and Partnership: the continual process in which species exchange energy and resources.

CHAPTER

RIGHTNESS OF SIZE

THE PROPORTIONS OF LIVING SYSTEMS—THEIR BIGNESS OR SMALLNESS
AND THEIR BUILT-IN LIMITATIONS TO GROWTH—THAT INFLUENCE A
SYSTEM'S STABILITY AND SUSTAINABILITY

Nature favors the right size for all. A giraffe is tall, a mouse is small, and each size offers its own advantages. The 20th-century British anthropologist and biologist Gregory Bateson encouraged his students to consider "optimum size" and to "think as Nature thinks." He even wrote a modern-day fable, "The Tale of the Polyploid Horse," in which a great scientist creates a big horse. He wanted it to be exactly twice the size of an ordinary Clydesdale—twice as long and twice as high and twice as thick. As a colt, the horse could stand on its own four legs, but as it grew, its weight became eight times as much as a normal Clydesdale. Every morning the scientist had to raise the horse to its feet with a crane and suspend the animal in a box with

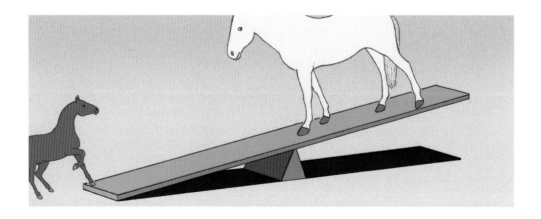

wheels and springs to take off half its weight. The horse also had a hard time keeping cool, since its skin and fat was twice as thick as it should be, yet its surface area was only four times that of an ordinary horse. The horse had to spend its days in a water bath just to keep its temperature normal. Rather than creating a bigger, better horse, the scientist created a horse twice its size with twice the problems.

With this cautionary tale, Bateson illustrated that in nature animals and other living systems thrive not by maximizing but by optimizing, that is, not by growing bigger but by growing better. Is his fable so preposterous? Perhaps not. Some dog breeders, after all, have bred larger and larger dogs until they have produced huge dogs with weak joints.

The next time you hear that "bigger is better" ask yourself, *What size is appropriate?* and *What will change if the size shrinks or grows?* Sometimes, small is beautiful and sometimes, large is lovely, but just the right size is always perfect. This folktale from Turkey illustrates the principle of right, or optimal, size.

The Tale of the Pumpkin Vines & the Walnut Tree

Nasreddin Hodja sat under a walnut tree, fanning himself with a pumpkin leaf. "Oh, how hot my poor head is! I wonder if I dare take off this turban?" He looked around and decided no one was close enough to laugh at his baldness. So he unwound his turban and wiped his dripping hot head. He sighed contentedly as the breeze from his pumpkin-leaf fan blew on his smooth glistening head.

The Hodja was the sort of man who usually felt the urge to talk to someone. He enjoyed telling others of his exploits and giving advice. But, as he had determined, no one was close by. He could hear the tinkle of sheep bells and the reedy whine of a shepherd's flute on the distant hillside, but not a person could he see.

That did not stop the Hodja, however, for before long he turned to the walnut tree, shook an accusing finger, and said, "You silly old tree! Is that the best you can do? And that? And that?" The Hodja pointed scornfully at the walnuts growing on the tree.

"Look at the size of you! Aren't you ashamed?" The Hodja shook his fist at the tree. "You rise up so proud and high, but what do you have to brag about—just some little walnuts no bigger than my two thumbs. Take a lesson from your neighbor, the pumpkin vine. It lies along the ground, so humble and unimportant, but just look at the size of those golden pumpkins." The more he thought about it, the more disgusted the Hodja became with a world that made little walnuts grow on a noble tree and huge pumpkins grow on a crawling vine.

"Now, if I had been planning it," cried the Hodja to his audience of walnuts and pumpkins, "it would have been very different! The big important pumpkins would be waving proudly on the strong branches of this big important tree. The little unimportant walnuts could cling without any trouble to the spineless pumpkin vine. The vine might even hold up its head a little, if it had something the right size growing on it."

Unnoticed by him, a gentle breeze began swaying the branches above his bald bare head.

"Yes, yes," he went on, "if I had been in charge … "

The Hodja never finished his sentence. There was a little snap on the branch above his head, and something rushed through the leaves and, with a resounding smack, hit Hodja on his bald head.

For a minute the Hodja swayed. He saw little bright lights where none had been be fore. With his left hand he picked up a walnut—small, to be sure, but hard, oh, very hard. With his right hand he rubbed his poor head where a lump the size of a walnut was quickly rising.

Meekly, he said, "Oh, Allah. Forgive me for questioning the way pumpkins grow on vines and walnuts grow on trees. You were wiser than I. Just suppose a pumpkin had fallen from that tree onto my poor head!"

Holding his bruised and aching head, the Hodja stood and took a closer look at the beautiful golden pumpkins on their graceful vine. They were so close to the Earth that they could not possibly fall anywhere. Allah was wise. Allah be praised.

For centuries the folklore of Nasreddin Hodja has entertained the Turkish people. Here, the Hodja learns about the rightness to the sizes in nature. Walnuts the size of pumpkins? Pumpkins the size of walnuts? In nature, growth is controlled by a species and its environment. The thickness of a palm tree doesn't increase as the tree grows taller. If it grows more than its nomal height, it topples over. Along with the Hodja, we can learn to see if the size of something serves its purpose, or if it serves some other purpose, like status, profit, or ego.

Rightness of Size: The proportions of living systems–their bigness or smallness and their built-in limitations to growth–that influence a system's stability and sustainability.

CHAPTER

THE COMMONS

SHARED RESOURCES—SUCH AS AIR, WATER, LAND, HIGHWAYS, FISHERIES,
ENERGY, AND MINERALS—ON WHICH WE DEPEND AND FOR WHICH WE
ARE ALL RESPONSIBLE

Would you rather have cleaner air or more cars on the road? More parks and open fields or more shopping markets? Would you want more neighbors willing to watch your house when you go away or more locks on your doors? Most of us would choose "the commons"—those shared resources such as land, air, water, fisheries, minerals, libraries, even human knowledge and neighborliness on which we all depend and for which we are all responsible. Unfortunately, as the Greek philosopher Aristotle recognized long ago, "What is common to the greatest number gets the least amount of care."

If an activity or resource is open to all, then it is likely to be a commons. We are all free to visit a public park, walk on a city

sidewalk, or breathe the air. Some commons, such as the Sun, music, and language, are unlimited. Others, such as fisheries, energy, and schools, are limited or finite. They can be used up or overrun. With finite commons, we ask, How can we maintain and support our commons? One answer lies in everyone following certain rules to care for the commons and managing the commons for the long-term benefit of all. Then, as Aldo Leopold envisioned in his *Sand County Almanac* (1949), "we may begin to use [the commons] with love and respect."

In this Bini Nigerian folktale, a first people discovers that even the sky is a precious, common resource.

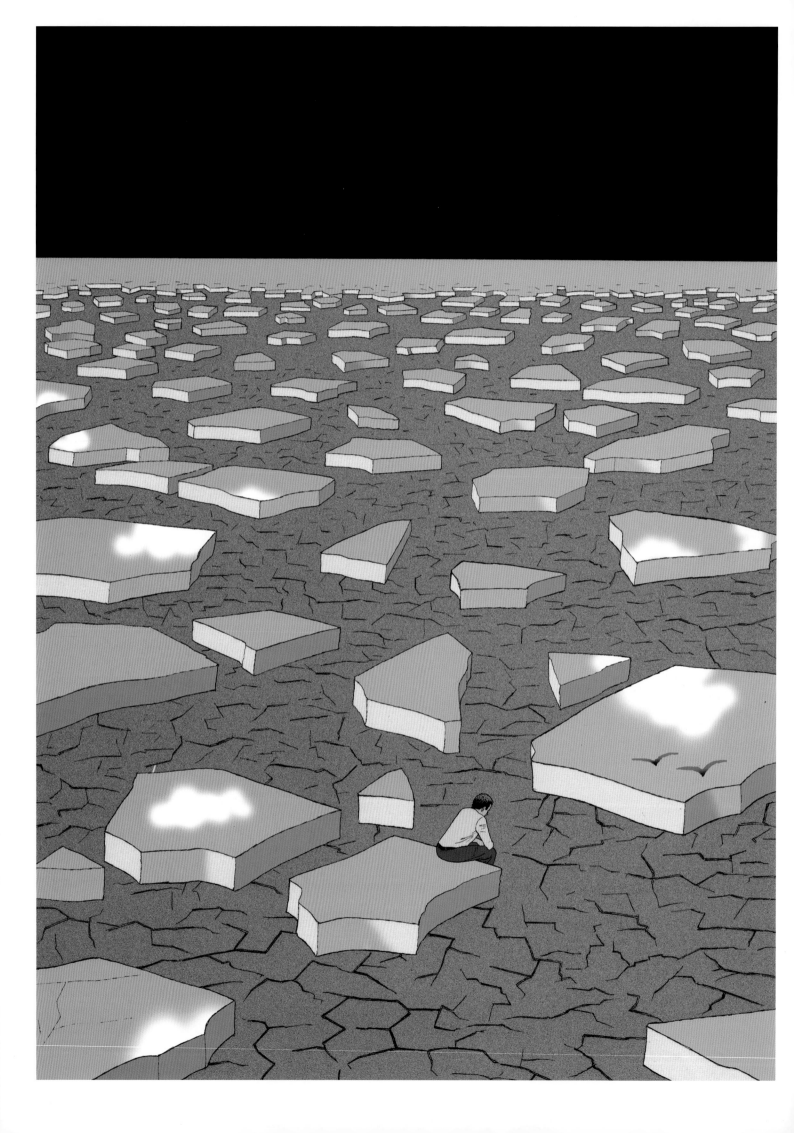

Too Much Sky

In the beginning, when Earth was very young, Sky came down and lovingly brushed Earth. In those days people didn't have to till the ground, because whenever they felt hungry, they reached up and cut off a piece of Sky and ate it.

This went on for many years until Sky grew angry because often people cut off more than they could eat and threw what was left on their rubbish heap. "If you're not more careful," Sky warned, "I'm going to move far away."

For a while everyone paid attention to Sky's warning. But then one day, a greedy woman cut off an enormous piece of Sky. She ate as much as she could but was unable to finish it. Frightened, she called her husband to help her. But he, too, couldn't finish it. Together, they called the entire village to help, but even with everyone helping, they couldn't finish it. In the end, they had to throw the remainder on the rubbish heap.

Sky said, "That's it, that's enough!" and rose up high above Earth, far beyond the reach of all the people. From then on, everyone had to work for their living, plowing the fields and hunting in the forest.

This folktale from the Bini of Nigeria can be read in many ways. It's a creation story about why the sky is far away, and it's a fable about what happens when self-restraint falls away and greed creeps in. We can also think of "Why the Sky Is Far Away" as a cautionary tale about the commons. When it comes to our commons, like our waterways, our air, the fish in our oceans, why do we find ourselves, as the greedy woman, acting destructively? Perhaps it has to do with not seeing our common resources as limited. As the American author and policy analyst Jonathan Rowe has written, "Before we can reclaim the commons, we have to remember how to see it." The sky gives us oxygen to breathe, protects us from ultraviolet rays, and regulates the Earth's temperature, and yet we do not protect it, because we do not see it as limited. When we see that the sky is a commons, we understand that we must all take care of it.

The Commons: Shared resources—such as air, water, land, highways, fisheries, energy, or minerals—on which we depend and for which we are all responsible.

CHAPTER

LIVING CYCLES

CIRCULAR PROCESSES THAT REPEAT OVER AND OVER, FREQUENTLY RETURNING TO WHERE THEY BEGAN. THE WATER, LUNAR, SLEEP, AND OTHER CYCLES SUSTAIN LIFE, CIRCULATE RESOURCES, AND PROVIDE OPPORTUNITIES FOR RENEWAL.

Everything in nature moves in cycles. Water lilies open their fragrant blossoms with the rise of the morning sun, then close their petals at dusk. Summer follows spring, winter follows autumn. Water, nitrogen, carbon, and even rocks follow cycles.

While we may not think much about natural cycles, we often disrupt them. When we pave streets and parking lots, we interrupt the water cycle by lessening the amount of water absorbed into the soil and increasing the amount of water diverted into storm sewers. When we reach for a cup of coffee in the afternoon because we feel tired, we ignore the body's signal to wind down and prepare for the rest part of the sleep cycle. By meddling with our sleep cycle, we become more tired, no matter how much coffee we drink.

When we pay attention to natural cycles, we discover that they offer a gift: Undisturbed cycles bring renewal. Farmers know this. After the harvest, autumn and winter bring a time of much-needed dormancy, allowing plants to decay and produce nutrients such as nitrogen, calcium, and carbon that make it possible for new crops to grow again in the spring.

How can we avoid disturbing natural cycles? Perhaps the first step is to recognize and respect them. This could involve something as simple as building more parks in our cities, or sleeping when we feel tired.

In the Sufi Tunisian folktale, "The Tale of the Sands," a stream discovers its own essential role in the water cycle.

The Tale of the Sands

Once, long ago, when streams and deserts and winds could talk, a trickling stream began its journey from a hidden place in the far-off mountains. It flowed on and on until it came to the desert. On its journey it crossed many barriers, but when the stream tried to cross the desert, it realized it could not. It just disappeared in the sand. *How can I get across the sands?* the stream wondered.

The stream was convinced that it was meant to cross this desert, yet there was no way. Just then a hidden voice, coming from the desert itself, whispered: "The wind crosses the desert, and so can you, stream."

"Of course the wind can cross. It can fly. But I only get absorbed when I try."

"It is true that by hurtling in your own accustomed way you will never get across. You will either disappear or become a marsh. You must allow the wind to carry you over to your destination."

"But how could this happen?"

The desert whispered, "By allowing yourself to disappear in the wind."

"Oh, no. I cannot allow that to happen! I would be lost forever. Then, how could I ever become a stream again?"

"Don't worry," the voice replied. "Wind takes you up, carries you over the desert, and lets you fall again as rain. Then you will once again become a river."

"But how do I know this is true?"

The wind replied, "If you do not believe me, you cannot become more than a quagmire, and even that may take many, many years."

The stream whimpered, "But I want to remain the same stream that I am today."

"What part of you is the essential one?" the whisper asked.

The stream thought it heard echoes, then, of other voices. They told it of another time, long ago, when he had been held in the arms of another wind. "Your essential part is carried away and forms a stream again."

So the stream raised his vapor into the welcoming arms of the wind, which gently and easily bore it upward and along, letting it fall softly as soon as they reached the roof of a mountain, many, many miles away. And because he had his doubts, the stream was able to remember and record more strongly in his mind the details of the experience. He thought, *Yes, now I have learned my true identity.*

The sands whispered. "We know, because we see it happen day after day, and because we, the sands, extend from the riverside all the way to the mountain."

And that is why it is said that the way in which the stream of life is to continue on its journey is written in the sands.

In the ever-present water cycle, water flows from the smallest creek to the largest lakes, finding its way eventually to the ocean. The water reenters the atmosphere as a vapor and then comes again to the land as rain, snow, and hail. In this Sufi tale, the stream learns to give itself over to the natural rhythm of the water cycle. Age-old wisdom tells us that when we embrace and even take advantage of natural cycles, we may discover new life rhythms of our own. When we don't understand natural cycles, sometimes our solutions become the problem.

Living Cycles: A cycle is a circular process that repeats over and over, frequently returning to where it began. The water, lunar, sleep and other cycles sustain life, circulate resources, and provide opportunities for renewal.

CHAPTER

WASTE = FOOD

WHEN WASTE FROM ONE SYSTEM BECOMES FOOD FOR ANOTHER. ALL
MATERIALS IN NATURE ARE VALUABLE, CONTINUOUSLY CIRCULATING IN
CLOSED LOOPS OF PRODUCTION, USE, AND RECYCLING.

If you've ever gone to pick berries, you've probably knocked a few good berries to the ground while trying to reach for that next perfect fruit. "What a waste!" you might find yourself thinking, as another loose berry hits the ground. Fortunately, nature doesn't create any extra waste. The bush's bounty is actually useful. The fruit on the ground, and the blossoms before it, return to the soil and become food for the plant itself. As American natural science writer Janine Benyus puts it: "All waste is food, and everybody winds up reincarnated inside somebody else."

Unfortunately, the human approach to waste tends to be more of a straight line that looks like this: Take → Make → Waste. We *take* raw materials, such as copper, iron, and minerals from

the Earth. We make goods, for example, cars, refrigerators, and computers. And then, because most of these products end up in the dump, where they cannot be put to use by anything or anyone, we waste. Even worse, when we *make* those products, we create more waste in the process, in the form of energy, solids, liquids, and gases that go unused. About 85% of the materials we use to manufacture goods also become *waste*.

We don't have to create unusable waste. If we imitate living systems, waste from one system can become "food" for another. Old tires can become shoes, plastic bottles can turn into fleece jackets, the remains of coffee plants can be used to grow mushrooms, and paper can become kitty litter or animal bedding. If thought through, waste equals food … for someone.

In the Sufi folktale from Syria "The Food of Paradise," a teacher discovers that the discarded waste of one can be the precious food of another.

The Food of Paradise

Long ago, a teacher named Yunus decided one day to figure out how it was that people got enough food to eat. I am a man, he said to himself, and as man I get a portion of the world's goods every day. This portion comes to me by my own efforts and with the help of many others. By simplifying this process, I shall find how and why sustenance comes to mankind. I shall throw myself upon the direct support of Allah and the power which rules over all.

So Yunus, trusting the support of invisible forces, began walking across the countryside. When night came, he fell asleep, certain that Allah would take care of his needs, just as the birds and animals were cared for in their own habitats.

At dawn the bird chorus awakened him, and Yunus lay still at first, waiting for his food to appear. In spite of his faith, he soon realized that his faith alone would not help him in his quest.

Lying on the riverbank, Yunus spent the whole day peering at the fish in the waters and saying his prayers. From time to time, rich and powerful men rode by on fine horses, harness bells jingling to signal their right of way. Parties of pilgrims paused and chewed dry bread and cheese. Yunus grew hungrier and hungrier.

This is but a test of my faith, Yunus thought. Soon all will be well. And he wrapped himself in contemplation for the fifth prayer of the day.

Another night passed. When morning came, Yunus stared at

the Sun's broken rays reflected in the Tigris. There he spotted a packet wrapped in palm leaves, bobbing in the reeds. He waded into the river to pick up this unusual cargo. Holding it carefully, he judged it to weigh about three-quarters of a pound. As he unwrapped it, a delicious almond aroma caressed his nose. It was halwa—a delicacy made from almond paste, rosewater and honey and prized for its sustaining and health-giving powers.

"My faith has been rewarded!" exclaimed Yunus.

For the next three days, Yunus sat at on the riverbank and waited. Sure enough, at exactly the same hour each day, a packet of halwa floated into his eager hands.

Surely now, he thought, I can figure out where this wonderful food comes from. Once I arrive at its source, I can teach others, for has it not been said "When you know, you must teach?"

For many days, Yunus followed the stream. Each day with the same regularity, but at a time correspondingly earlier, the halwa appeared, and he ate it. Eventually Yunus noticed that the river, instead of narrowing at the upper part, had widened considerably. In the middle of the water was an island upon which stood a mighty castle. "Surely, this must be the source of my halwa," Yunus said.

Just then a tall, unkempt dervish with matted hair, wearing a multicolored cloak, appeared before him.

"Peace, Baba, Father," Yunus said.

"Ishq, Hoo!" shouted the hermit. "And what is your business here?"

"I am on a sacred quest," exclaimed Yunus, "and I must reach yonder castle. Have you any idea how I might do this?"

"So, you are interested in this castle? I will tell you about it. The daughter of a king lives here. She is imprisoned by the man she refused to marry. Although she is attended by many beautiful servants, many invisible barriers keep her in her prison."

"Can you help me free her?"

The hermit looked deeply into Yunus's eyes. "First you must practice the Wazifa—the reciting of the 99 names of Allah. Then, if you are worthy, you will be able to summon the invisible powers of the Jinns." Yunus knew that the Jinns were the magical creatures of fire. "They alone can unlock the castle." Upon saying this, the old man moved away, much faster than someone his age should be able to move. In the distance, Yunus heard him say, "Upon you, peace."

Yunus did as the hermit instructed. One evening, as he looked at the setting sun shining upon a turret of the castle, he saw, shimmering with unearthly beauty, a woman. The princess. As she looked into the sun, she dropped a packet into the water below: halwa. Here, then, was the source of his bounty!

Yunus was overjoyed at finding this source of the Food of Paradise, and he recited the Wazifa and called upon the Jinns. They carried him up, up, up to where he met an ageless creature. "I am the Commander of the Jinns, and I have had thee carried here in answer to the words of the Great Dervish. What can I do for thee?"

Yunus trembled. "I am a seeker of the truth, and the answer to it is only to be found in the enchanted castle there. Give me, I pray, the power to enter this castle and talk to the imprisoned princess."

"So shall it be!" exclaimed the commander. "But," he warned, "a man gets an answer to his questions in accordance with his fitness to understand."

"Truth is truth," said Yunus, "and I will have it, no matter what it may be."

The Commander of the Jinns then gave Yunus a mirror-stone that could show him the castle's hidden defenses. Soon Yunus found himself speeding along, accompanied by a band of Jinns charged by their commander to aid this human on his quest.

By looking through the stone, Yunus could see that the castle was protected by a row of giants, invisible but terrible, who stood ready to kill anyone who approached. But the Jinns cleared them away in a flash. Next, Yunus found an invisible net hanging all around the castle. This, too, the flying Jinns destroyed. Finally, they encountered an invisible mass of stone, which filled the entire space between the castle and the riverbank. But the Jinns quickly broke through the stone barrier. Their mission accomplished, they saluted Yunus and flew fast as light back to their abode.

Yunus, standing all alone, saw that a bridge had emerged from the riverbed. He could walk with dry feet to the castle, where he was met by a soldier who took him immediately to the princess. She was even more beautiful than Yunus had imagined.

"We are grateful to you for destroying the defenses of this prison," said the lady. "I may now return to my father, but first I want to reward you. Name it, and it shall be yours."

"Beautiful lady," said Yunus, "there is only one thing which I seek, and that is truth."

"Speak, and such truth will freely be yours."

"Very well, your highness. How is it that the Food of Paradise, the wonderful halwa which you throw out every day, comes to me?"

The princess smiled and said, "Oh, Yunus, the halwa, as you call it, is what is left from my cosmetics and lotions after my daily bath of donkey's milk. I simply throw it away."

"I have at last learned," said Yunus, "that the understanding of a man is conditional upon our capacity to understand. For you, the packet contains the remains of your daily bath. For me, it is the Food of Paradise."

Yunus was a Syrian who died in 1670. It is said he was an innovator with extraordinary healing powers. In this adaptation of a Sufi tale (originally told by Sufi author Halqavi), Yunus sets out to discover the divine source of human sustenance. He discovers a simple principle that guides all living systems: one inhabitant's waste can become another's food.

Waste = Food: When waste from one system becomes food for another. All materials in nature are valuable, continuously circulating in closed loops of production, use, and recycling.

CHAPTER

BALANCING FEEDBACK

CIRCULAR PROCESSES THAT CREATE STABILITY BY COUNTERACTING OR
LESSENING CHANGE

Have you ever been out in the cold so long that you started to shiver? By shaking your muscles, shivering warms your body back up to its normal 37°C (98.6°F). Have you ever been so hot that you became soaked with sweat? When you're too hot, sweating cools your body back down to 37°. Shivering and sweating are part of a particular pattern of interaction, called balancing feedback, that enables any living system to thrive in the face of outside changes or threats. Balancing feedback works to keep living systems in a state of dynamic balance through an endless series of self-correcting changes.

We see balancing feedback in action throughout nature with the relationship between a predator and its prey. When one popula-

tion starts to increase in numbers, zebras for example, the population that preys on it (such as lions) also grows. Over time, as more and more lions are able to survive, there are fewer zebras. With less food, the predator population begins to decline. Eventually, the prey population increases, and balance is restored.

By its very nature, balancing feedback works to bring things to a desired state and keep them there. We often see this pattern in everyday situations, such as trying to keep a living area neat. We can think of it like this: A parent asks his or her child to clean up a messy area → child cleans area → parent is happy → the pressure to clean is off → the area gets messy once again. We also see balancing feedback in efforts to maintain a steady supply of qualified doctors. Hospital administrators, for instance, describe the pressures they experience around supply and demand of medical staff. When demand for doctors goes up, more people go to medical school, leading to an oversupply of doctors. When physicians find it difficult to get jobs, fewer people go into the profession, and hospitals experience staffing shortages.

In the balancing feedback around us, we see that the process always has a goal, some point of balance the system seeks. When we pay attention to balancing feedback in our everyday lives, we begin to wonder: What is the goal here? What does balance in this system look like? We find ourselves better able to anticipate resistance and occasionally learn to reset the goal.

In this tale from the Penobscots, a native people of North America, young Gluskabe upsets the balance of the forest animals, but with the help of his wise grandmother, is able to see both his goal and the error of his ways.

Gluskabe Traps the Animals

One day, Gluskabe went out to hunt. He tried hunting in the woods, but the game animals were not to be seen. Hunting is slow, he thought, so he returned to the wigwam where he lived with his grandmother Woodchuck. He lay down on his bed and began to sing: "I wish for a game bag, I wish for a game bag … to make it easier to hunt."

He repeated his song so many times that his grandmother said, "All right! I'll make you a game bag of deer hair. Now, stop singing!"

But he kept singing. "I wish for a game bag … " over and over, until Grandmother made him a game bag of caribou hair. Still he continued to sing, "I wish for a game bag, I wish for a game bag … to make it easier to hunt."

This time Grandmother Woodchuck crafted a game bag of moose hair. "Here, Gluskabe. Now will you stop singing and go hunting?" Still Gluskabe sang: "I wish for a game bag, I wish for a game bag, I wish for a game bag … of Woodchuck hair!"

Being the loving grandmother that she was, she plucked hair from her belly and made him a game bag. Gluskabe sat up and stopped singing. "Thank you, Grandmother," he said.

He went into the forest and called the animals. "Come," he said. "The world is going to end, and all of you will die. Get into my game bag, and you will not see the end of the world."

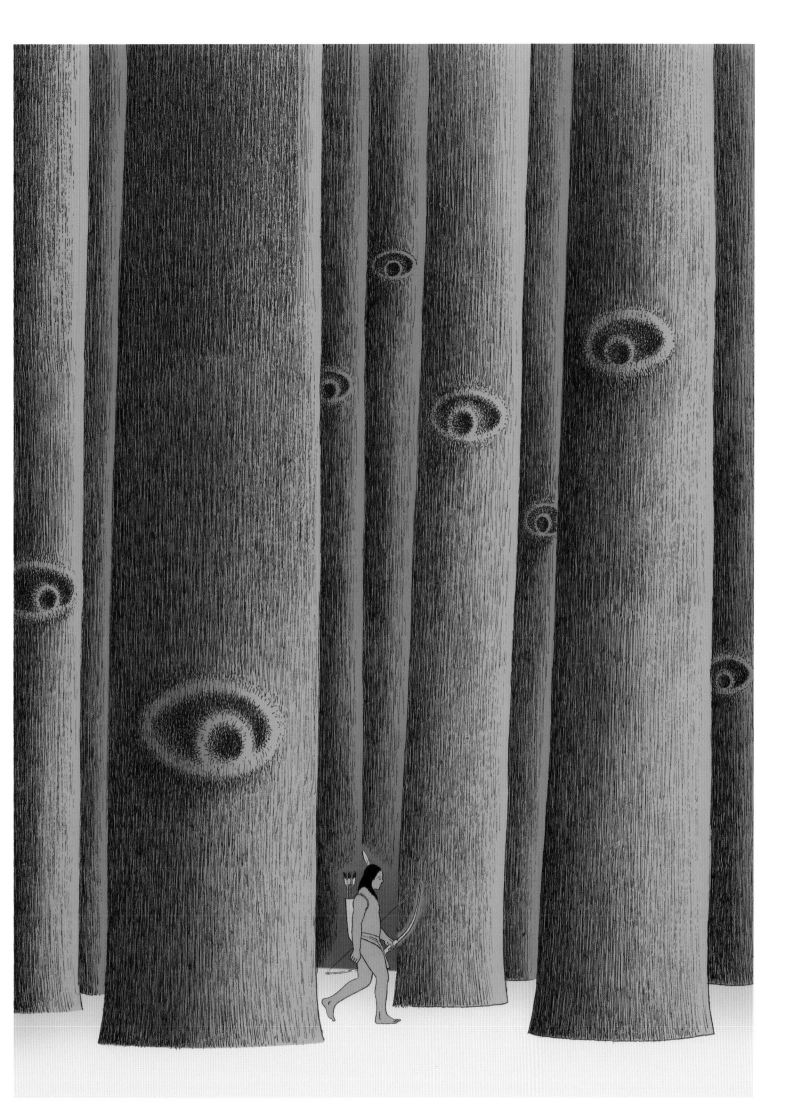

Then all of the animals came out of the forest and ran into Gluskabe's game bag. One by one they came in great numbers: the squirrels, the rabbits, the muskrats, the raccoons, the porcupines, the deer, and the bears. The bag stretched and stretched until it held all the animals. Gluskabe closed the bag and ran all the way back to his grandmother's wigwam.

"Grandmother, I tricked all the game animals into climbing into my bag. Now we will not have a hard time hunting."

Grandmother Woodchuck saw all the animals in the game bag. "You have not done well, Grandson," she said. "In the future, our small ones, our children's children, will die of hunger without these animals. You must not do this. You must do what will help our children's children."

Gluskabe thought about her words. Finally, he got up and said, "I want my children's children to live with animals, too. But it is hard work to hunt for food."

"Yes, it is," Grandmother Woodchuck said. "But you will become wiser and learn that if you take too many animals, there will not be enough for all. If you take just enough, the animals will have plenty of children. There will be a good balance this way."

So Gluskabe went back into the forest with his game bag. He opened it. "Go, the danger is past," he said. Then the animals came out of the game bag and scattered throughout the forest. This is the end of my story.

For the native peoples of northeastern North America, Gluskabe is a mythical hero who helps create the world, among other things. In this tale, young Gluskabe learns about the consequences of interrupting nature's dynamic balance. Taking too many game animals means there will be fewer animals to regenerate their numbers, which results in fewer animals for all the hunters for years to come. Like Gluskabe, we can be wise and learn to understand the balancing feedback processes all around us.

Balancing Feedback: circular processes that create stability by counteracting or lessening change.

66

CHAPTER

REINFORCING FEEDBACK

CIRCULAR PROCESSES THAT CREATE GROWTH OR DECAY BY AMPLIFYING
OR REINFORCING CHANGE

Have you ever heard someone say, "We're on a roll!" when successes seem to build on themselves, or "We're spiraling out of control!" when problems continue to pile up? When people use these kinds of phrases, they tend to be describing reinforcing feedback, a circular process in which a change builds on itself over time.

The expression *vicious cycle*, for example, suggests rapidly building momentum in a negative direction. A teacher might describe a student whose low self-esteem and poor performance are reinforcing each other as being in a *downward spiral*. A biologist might use a different term, such as *cascading*, to describe events that trigger other events in an ever-growing spiral, for example the growth of an embryo from a single cell. A climatolo-

gist might discuss the reinforcing effect of a slight rise in over-all atmospheric temperature, which is currently occurring. This increase has caused ice to melt in polar regions; the now bare ground absorbs more heat, causing even more ice to melt.

Reinforcing feedback can also be a good thing. We experience this engine of positive growth in many situations, for example when learning builds on previous learning, or compound interest helps our bank account to grow, or when we see one act of kindness lead to another. Whether reinforcing feedback consists of an engine of growth or decay, we can work with it and even change the hidden forces that cause it.

In Aesop's fable "Hercules and Pallas," mighty Hercules finds himself caught in an escalating spiral of aggression.

Hercules and Pallas

Hercules, once journeying along a narrow roadway, came across a strange-looking animal that reared its head and threatened him. Never daunted, the hero gave him a few lusty blows with his club, thinking he would set it on its way.

The monster, however, much to the astonishment of Hercules, was now three times as big as it was before, and all the more threatening. He thereupon redoubled his blows and laid about him fast and furiously, but the harder and quicker the strokes of the club, the bigger and more frightful grew the monster, and now completely filled up the road.

The goddess of wisdom, Pallas then appeared upon the scene. "Stop, Hercules," she said. "Cease your blows. The monster's name is Strife. Let it alone, and it will soon become as little as it was at first."

"Strife feeds on conflict."

Until Pallas appears, Hercules does not see how he and Strife are trapped in a reinforcing feedback loop. The greater Hercules' aggression, the larger Strife grows, and the larger Strife grows, the greater Hercules' aggression. Hercules is caught up in an escalation, a type of reinforcing feedback loop in which one party does something that is seen as a threat by another party, causing the other party to respond in kind and so increasing the perception of threat to the first party. This results in a rising spiral of aggression. It is only when Hercules realizes, with the help of Pallas, he must not respond, that the spiral is broken.

Reinforcing feedback: circular loops of mutual causality that amplify change. Sometimes known as "escalation," also as "vicious" or "virtuous" cycles.

CHAPTER

NONLINEARITY

A TYPE OF BEHAVIOR IN WHICH THE EFFECT IS
DISPROPORTIONATE TO THE CAUSE

W e humans tend to think linearly, that is, that results occur in equal proportion to the force applied. After all, a small turn of the volume on one's radio results in a small change in the volume, and some pressure on the gas pedal of a car results in an equal increase in speed.

But many things do not operate in a linear manner. Traffic jams, weather patterns, and epidemics are additional examples of nonlinearities. In living systems the puzzling behavior associated with nonlinear phenomena emerges not out of a series of straight lines of cause and effect but out of myriad interconnections, feedback loops, and networks. Within these twisty, curvy, loopy interconnections, even the slightest change can have enormous and disproportionate effects.

The urban crime-fighting method of "fix one broken window" is another example of nonlinearity. Addressing small crimes (such as broken windows and graffiti) can set off nonlinear change. For instance, New York City officials found that fixing broken windows in city neighborhoods reduced crime. Repairing the windows and restoring the visual appeal of a street created a greater sense of order and a feeling of safety in the neighborhood surrounding it, leading more people to spend time outside. More families outdoors meant more adult supervision of the street, which further lowered crime and increased the community's overall sense of safety and order. One small change in this living system we call a city neighborhood set in motion a much larger set of consequences.

When we come to grasp the nonlinearities in all living systems—including our oceans, our backyards, our families, and our communities—we begin to see these systems as exquisitely sensitive and vulnerable to what happens in every other part of the system. We also remember that owing to the nature of living systems, results are frequently disproportionate to events. Big changes can be produced from very small actions, as in fixing a broken window on a city street, and large actions can sometimes have very small or unintended effects, as in the use of agricultural pesticides, where the pesticides in the end have little effect on the pests because they are killing off natural predators and stimulating the evolution of pesticide-resistant pests and weeds.

In the timeless Burmese folktale "A Kingdom Lost for a Drop of Honey," a king discovers the consequences of a single stray drop of honey.

A Kingdom Lost for a Drop of Honey

One day, the king and his chief adviser stood by the open palace window, looking out onto the street below. They were having such a good time. They laughed and talked as they snacked on rice and honey. At one point, the king chuckled so hard that he spilled a drop of honey on the windowsill.

"Allow me to wipe that up for you, your majesty," said the adviser. "Do not bother," said the king. "It is just a drop of honey. We have servants to take care of such things. Spilling need not concern *us*."

So they continued to talk and eat and laugh. They did not notice that the drop of honey fell onto the street below. Soon a fly landed on the honey and began a feast of its own. And before long a lizard spied the fly, pounced, and swallowed the fly whole. The lizard did not notice a cat slinking along in the shadows of the palace. Suddenly, she leaped forward and swallowed the lizard. Then when the cat sat down to digest her dinner in the sun, a dog suddenly sprang out and attacked her.

All of this made a great deal of noise. "Sire, should we send someone to stop this fight?" asked the adviser. "Do not bother," said the king. "It does not concern *us*."

So they kept on eating and talking. Meanwhile, the owner of the cat arrived on the scene. He picked up a stick and began to beat the dog. But just at that instant, the owner of the dog appeared. He grabbed a stick and began to beat the cat. It was

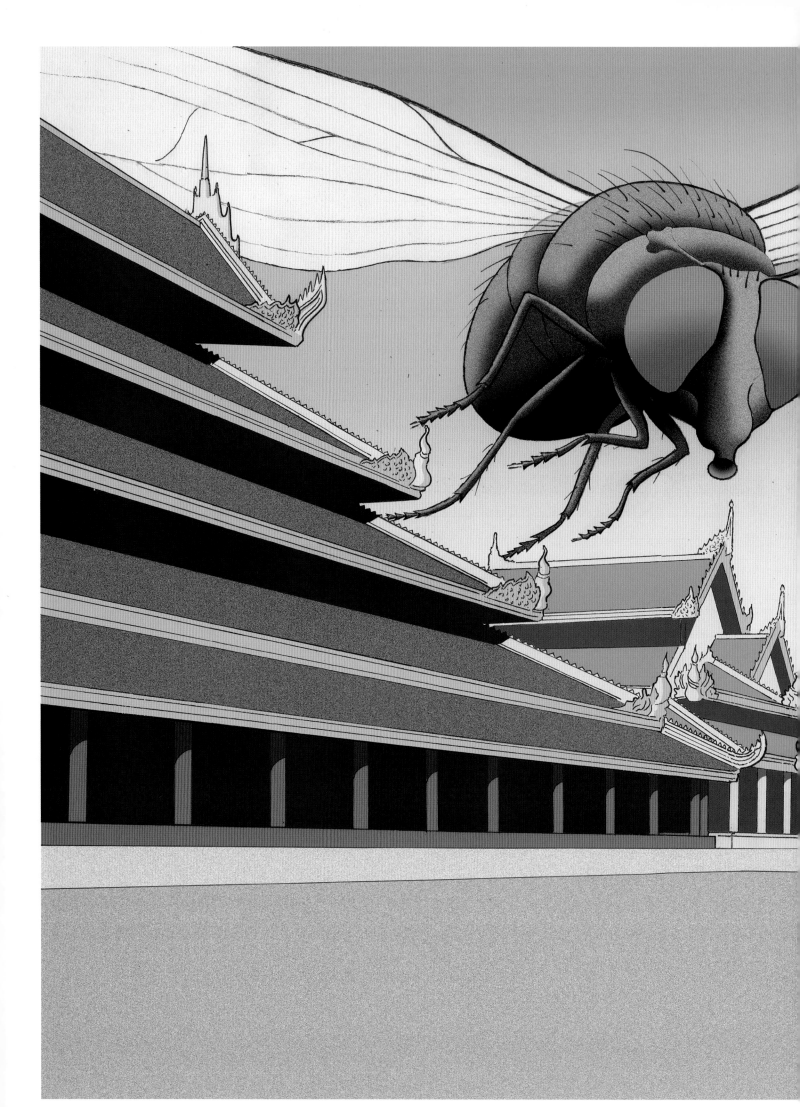

not long before the two men started hitting each other instead of the animals.

"Sire, now there are two men fighting down there on the street. Shall we order some guards to put an end to it?" asked the adviser.

The king stopped eating and looked down at the commotion in the street. "Do not bother. It does not concern *us*."

The fight gathered onlookers. Some people sided with the cat owner, others with the dog owner. Soon the two groups attacked each other.

"Sire, I fear things are getting worse," cried the adviser. "Now large groups of people are fighting. Should we not try to stop it?" The king just took another bite of rice and honey and said, "Do not bother. It does not concern *us*."

Soldiers soon arrived to put an end to the fighting. But when they heard the cause of the fight, they took sides as well. Once the soldiers got involved, it turned into a full-blown civil war! Houses were burned down, and many people were injured. It was not long before the flames spread to the palace, and it, too, burned to the ground. The king looked at the ruins of his palace and admitted, "I guess I was wrong. That drop of honey did concern *us*."

It took many years for the king to rebuild his palace. From then on, he was a much wiser leader who always listened carefully to others. He never forgot that even the smallest act can have great consequences.

Nonlinearity may sound like a fancy new term, yet it is an ancient truth that we see expressed in various cultures and languages around the world. The Chinese capture nonlinearity in this simple proverb: "An ant may well destroy a whole dam." The Arabic proverb "the straw that broke the camel's back" and the French proverb "little brooks make great rivers" also illustrate the idea of disproportionate effect. In this tale the king overrides his chief adviser's intuition about the power of nonlinear phenomena. After all, what consequence could a single drop of honey have? He finds out that even the tiniest act can have enormous consequences, particularly when myriad interconnections and reinforcing loops of cause and effect are involved.

Nonlinearity: a type of behavior in which the effect is disproportionate to the cause.

CHAPTER

EARTH TIME

THE PACE OF THE BIOSPHERE, THAT IS, THE PACE AT WHICH LIFE OCCURS
FOR ALL LIVING ORGANISMS

When we plant vegetables in our garden, we know we have to wait weeks before the first green carrot tufts or pea vines appear. In one part of India, bamboo is planted 1.2 m (4 ft) underground. Farmers water the spot every day for two years without seeing any growth above ground. Then after two years, the bamboo shoots to 18.3 m (60 ft) high in 90 days. Whether we wait a few weeks for carrot tufts or two years for bamboo shoots, we can think of the time required for this growth as the pace of the biological world, or the biosphere.

Increasingly, the pace of the technological world, or technosphere, pushes us to adjust to—and to expect—faster and faster changes brought about by the newest technological innovation. We push a button on our computer and expect a package to show

up at our door the next day. Rather than sleeping, we can send and receive electronic files at two in the morning. As humans are pulled into the pace of the technosphere, we can become disconnected from the pace of the biosphere. Yet the biosphere, the source of life, deserves our attention and our patience. Many of our most vexing problems, such as climate change or the loss of biodiversity, have developed out of our lack of attention to processes occurring at the pace of the biosphere.

When we remember the pace of the biosphere—or Earth time— we remember that the pace of the industrial age is just one pace among many. We observe our responses to systems that appear to be slow moving. We take care not to overcorrect, oversteer, or worse, disregard those slow-moving systems. When we remember Earth time, we find ways to slow down so that our inner rhythms are attuned, as American ecophilosopher and educator Joanna Macy suggests, to "longer, ecological rhythms and nourish a strong, felt connection with past and future generations."

As the impatient farmer in the Chinese tale "The Rice Puller of Chaohwa" discovers, the length of time over which a living system develops may be longer than we are willing to wait.

The Rice Puller of Chaohwa

Once a farmer named Liu Always-In-A-Hurry lived near the village of Chaohwa. Every day Liu nagged at his wife and sons to "work faster!" And whenever he went into the village, he stepped on the heels of anyone on the path in front of him. Liu had an uncontrollable desire to be first in everything he did.

One day Liu heard a group of farmers talking about their rice fields. "My rice is sprouting very well," one of them said, "It is nearly two inches high."

Another farmer said, "Yes, my rice is doing well also. It is perhaps a little more than two inches high, nearly three."

"It is a good year for me, too," a third man said. "In some parts of my field the rice is nearly four inches tall already."

Liu knew his own rice was not four inches tall. Perhaps not even three. So he hurried back to his fields to measure his rice. Rushing, as usual, he, bumped into people along the way, and then he took a shortcut by tramping through a neighbor's rice paddy.

His heart fell when he reached his fields. His rice was barely two inches tall. He hurried home, pondering his problem. Ignoring his wife and sons, he went to bed, tossing and turning all night long. Then, just before dawn, he sat up and shouted, "I will help them!"

Without even eating breakfast, he ran to his fields, reached down, and took hold of one of the sprouts with his fingers. Then he pulled ever so gently. The sprout came up a little.

"Aha, that's better!" Liu said. Then he pulled the next stalk up a little, then the next. He went through the whole field this way, and by nightfall he returned home, weary and worn.

The next day he again rushed again to his fields and tugged at each rice plant. When he returned home at nightfall, he told his family: "Oh, I am tired! I worked so hard today! But the rice is much taller now, and I am happy!"

Liu's family was surprised at the news, for rice grows ever so slowly. So in the morning they went out together to see the result of Liu's hard work.

What they found was sad to see, for every single rice stalk lay withered and dead in the morning sun.

"Alas, is this gratitude?" Liu cried out to the ruined field. "Is this my reward for giving you a helping hand?"

As for the people of Chaohwa, when Liu's news got around, they laughed and laughed at the outcome of his impatience. And although Liu himself was forgotten as new generations were born and died in Chaohwa, to this very day people still say to someone who is overly eager: "Do not be a rice puller."

Most of us can't imagine pulling on rice stalks to make them grow faster. Yet we might expect to take a few guitar lessons and play like a rock star, or expect a group to work as a team after just a few days, or want efforts to reduce carbon emissions to have an effect immediately. We can learn from Earth's time, and Liu's experience, to take a longer view, to slow down, and to understand that sometimes the results of our actions lay in the distant future.

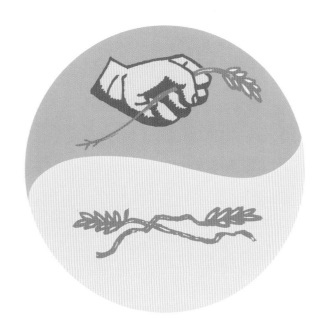

Earth time: the pace of the biosphere, that is, the pace at which life occurs for all living organisms.

APPENDIX A

MORE PRINCIPLES OF LIVING SYSTEMS

Where do we begin to change the way we view the world? How do we become more "systems literate" so that we can see the connections as well as the parts of any system?

To be literate means one has a good understanding of a particular subject, such as a foreign language or mathematics. In this case, the subject is living systems. When we become systems literate, we begin to make everyday decisions within the context of a deep understanding of living systems principles. We become less likely to blame a single cause for the challenges we encounter and, instead, make it a habit to trace complex interrelationships, knowing that there are no disconnected actions and that "actions leave tracks" (Chapter 1: "Interdependence").

We try to anticipate how the functioning of a living system will change if a part or a process is removed (Chapter 2: "Systems Integrity"). We seek diversity, knowing that the more diverse a community, the healthier, more resilient, and more flexible it is (Chapter 3: "Biodiversity"). We begin to understand the role different species and people play in the exchange of energy and resources (Chapter 4: "Cooperation and Partnership"). We look for closed loops of production, where waste from one source can be "food" for another (Chapter 8: "Waste = Food"). We begin to question the assumption that bigger is always better (Chapter 5: "Rightness of Size"). We become increasingly aware of those natural, shared gifts upon which we depend and for which we are all responsible (Chapter 6:"The Commons").

We learn to see recurring patterns that exist among a wide variety of systems (Chapter 7: "Living Cycles"). We use our understanding of those patterns to correct actions, anticipate intended consequences, and produce learning. Balancing feedback loops (Chapter 9: "Balancing Feedback"), for instance, produce continual fluctuations (as in our up-and-down sleep cycles or boom-and-bust cycles in the marketplace). When we understand reinforcing feedback (Chapter 10: "Reinforcing Feedback"), we look at how our "solutions" may actually be making the original problem worse.

As we become systems literate, we learn to optimize—or make as effective as possible—rather than maximize—or make the most of—those variables. When we become more aware of living systems, we see that consequences are not always proportionate to actions (Chapter 11: "Nonlinearity"). Our awareness of living systems also brings our attention to the Earth's or biosphere's pace of change, which can often be in stark contrast to that of the technosphere (Chapter 12: "Earth Time").

After conversations with many scientists and practitioners, I selected 12 principles of living systems to highlight in this book. There are, however, many other key concepts related to living systems and living sustainably. This appendix provides a summary of other key concepts of living systems. Where possible, I have included relevant folktales for these principles.

NETWORKS

Networks are complex sets of interconnections. They form a framework for how species in an ecosystem exchange resources, survive and thrive. Other terms sometimes used to describe networks in nature are *food chains* and *food webs* among others. While *interdependence* (Chapter 1) describes the relationships between and among species, network is a broader term that describes the pattern of organization created by interdependencies. Our nervous system is a complex, organized network of interconnections, as are a city's transportation system, our social relationships, and the World Wide Web.

EMERGENT PROPERTIES

We've probably all heard the adages "the whole is greater than the sum of its parts" or "one plus one equals three." When we are speaking about living systems, these old sayings become a good way to explain "emergent properties," or behavior that arises out of the interactions within a specific set of parts. Imagine taking your car completely apart. If you weighed all the pieces and added up the numbers, you'd know how much the entire car weighs when it is assembled correctly. But you wouldn't know how fast the car would go or how comfortable a ride you'd have on a bumpy road. Speed and comfort are created by the interactions of the car's parts and thus are "greater than the sum" of all separate parts of the car. When we lose sight of emergent properties, we can find ourselves maximizing the parts to the detriment of the whole.

NESTED SYSTEMS

Living systems are nested within one another other in many different ways: physically and spatially and also through time and space. For example, cells are nested within organisms, which are nested within ecosystems, which are nested within communities, which are nested within the Earth which is nested within the universe. When we understand that all systems are nested, we know there are no isolated entities. Then, when we wish to make a change to a system, we know that changes made to one part are not as likely to succeed as changes made at all levels of the nesting. For example, if improvements are needed in an educational system, changes must be made in the classroom, the school, and the community.

SELF-GENERATION, OR AUTOPOIESIS

Living systems create themselves through a process Chilean biologist Humberto Maturana termed "autopoiesis." Autopoietic systems are composed of a network of interactions that continually regenerate the elements and the network. For example, our bodies produce a whole new layer of skin cells every 28 days, and all cells in the body are replaced within seven years. The basic pattern of organization of the body is preserved, but the cells, interacting with the environment, are continually replaced. Living systems continually recreate themselves, whether a body or a community or an ecosystem. Social systems are continually re-created by their members through the reinforcing patterns of their interactions. Therefore, to be effective and enduring, change to any system must be self-created and re-created by the members of the system.

COGNITION AND LEARNING

Unlike mechanical systems, living systems are responsive to their environments. This enables a system to remain in harmony with an environment even as the environment changes. This capacity, called "structural coupling," holds the structure of the living system, determines its behavior, and must be in accord with the requirements of its environment in order for the system to survive. This view, based on the work of Chilean biologists Humberto Maturana and Francisco Varela, may also be considered a type of learning at a deep level. In this sense, the ability to learn continually is a necessary condition for a living system to thrive. This quality of cognition is one of the oldest questions in both Eastern and Western philosophy, although the concept is just beginning to be explored by science. The idea is not new to indigenous peoples, though; many folktales teach young people to be aware of the living forest (or lake or savannah), since it is alive and aware of them.

THE FIRST AND SECOND LAWS OF THERMODYNAMICS

Thermodynamics describes the movement of energy. As taught to secondary school physics students, the first law of thermodynamics tells us that the total amount of energy in the universe is constant. The second law tells us that matter and energy tend to spread and dissipate. When we understand these laws, we know that stuff, or matter, doesn't go away (the first law of thermodynamics), but it does get away (the second law of thermodynamics). How do these laws show up in our everyday lives? Anyone who owns a pet knows you find animal hair where the pet has never been. (The pet hair doesn't go away, but it does get away.) We find chemical plumes miles away from original sources, just as radioactive fallout from Chernobyl was found thousands of miles away in Sweden.

The "Slippers of Abu Kasem," an old Arabic story, is also ideal for introducing the second law of thermodynamics. As Abu Kasem comes to understand, there is no "away."

> Abu Kasem was a prosperous business man of Baghdad. He was very rich and very successful. He wore an old pair of slippers of which he was very fond. They were faded and

crooked and had been patched and mended so many times that they were the talk of every cobbler in the city. But no matter how worn they were, no matter how awful they looked, Abu Kasem always thought they were not so bad and that he could wear them a little longer. His friends would argue with him, pointing out what sorry things they were. And finally after a number of years, Abu Kasem decided to get rid of them.

One day in the public bath he put on a new pair and went home. But the bath attendants found the old ones, recognized them, and sent them to his house. Abu Kasem then threw them in the river. Some fishermen pulled them up in a net. They were angry because the nails in the slippers had torn the net, so they threw the dripping things in Abu Kasem's window and broke a valuable vase.

Nothing to do but bury them, he thought. So at night Abu slipped into the garden and buried them. A curious neighbor saw him and told the governor that Abu Kasem was burying treasure. This was a crime because discovered treasure belonged to the caliph. Abu protested that he had only buried an old pair of slippers. But nobody believed that, and Abu Kasem had to pay a heavy fine.

The next thing he did was to take the old slippers out into the country far from Baghdad and throw them in a pond. He did not know it was a city reservoir. The slippers got stuck in a pipe and stopped it up. Workmen went to the place to find out the trouble, found Abu Kasem's old slippers, recognized them, and reported him to the governor. Abu Kasem was fined again, this time for throwing rubbish in the city's water supply. He decided to burn the slippers. But first he put them on the balcony in the sun to dry. The dog found them and began to play with them. The dog tossed one in the air and over the balcony rail. It fell to the street below and hit a woman in the head. Abu Kasem was fined again. (Adapted from Maria Leach's *The Soup Stone: The Magic of Familiar Things* [New York: Funk & Wagnalls Co., 1954] pp. 96-97)

THE PARTS-WHOLE CONNECTION, OR THE SEED PRINCIPLE

In living systems the whole is not only composed of parts, but it is contained in the parts. For example, a simple cell contains all the information it needs to generate the whole organism when it interacts within an environment that contains the appropriate nutrients. An acorn holds the potential, when it interacts with the sun, soil, and water, to become a giant oak tree. The cell and the acorn may seem like parts, but in fact they are both places, as Henri Bortoft, German physicist and philosopher of science, put it, "for presencing the whole." When we understand this principle, we see our schools, our organizations, not as parts, but as seeds of potential interacting with larger environments.

CARRYING CAPACITY

Carrying capacity is a term used for the maximum number of species an area can support without causing deterioration to that area. For example, the carrying capacity of a savannah is the maximum number of animals that area can support without depleting the vegetation. If Earth's resources are finite, what is the carrying capacity for human beings in a given location on the planet? Just as we know how many children we can safely shuttle around in our car, or how many hikers can use a mountain trail without damaging it, we need to know the carrying capacity of our cities, towns, and villages and if we are living within that capacity.

The English folktale "The Three Green Ladies" is a good story for exploring the limits of Earth's carrying capacity. For a good read-aloud version of this story, see Margaret Read MacDonald's *Earth Care: World Folktales to Talk About* (North Haven, CT: Linnet Books,1999), pp.1-7.

FLUX

The 6th-century BCE Greek philosopher Heraclitus asked the simple question, What is reality made of? His answer was *panta rhei*, or "everything flows." Today, we call this "flux," or the continual movement of energy, matter, and information through living systems. Flux enables the living, or open, system to remain alive, flexible, and ever changing. The Sun, for instance, provides a constant flux, or flow of energy and resources, which sustains all living organisms. (This process, called photosynthesis, occurs when plants and other organisms convert sunlight into energy.) We see flux occur as energy passes through a food web and as ideas pass through an organization. When we understand flux, we understand why Heraclitus once proclaimed, "You can't step into the same river twice." We become suspect of any attempts at problem solving that assume the world stands still while it is being analyzed. Instead, as living systems thinkers, we see every living system as being in a continual state of change.

EXPONENTIAL, OR RUNAWAY, GROWTH

Runaway growth, also known as exponential growth, is a particular kind of reinforcing feedback (Chapter 10) in which the larger the quantity (for example, the amount of money in a bank account), the greater the rate of growth of that quantity. And then, as a result of this reinforcing process, we see an even greater quantity in the future. So why do most of us profoundly underestimate the effect of exponential growth? One answer may be that much of the expansion and change in our daily lives is linear; therefore, a great deal of our experience is with linear growth, not exponential growth. A linear process occurs when traveling in a car; you can assume you travel 80.5 km (50 mi) in distance for one hour on the road. An exponential process would, for example, double the speed every hour.

These reinforcing loops lie at the heart of exponential growth that we see around us every day: compounding interest, population growth, rising productivity, and even arms races between nations.

In the Indian folktale "Sissa and the Troublesome Trifles," a king asks his advisers to create a game that demonstrates the values of prudence, diligence, foresight, and knowledge. So pleased with the inventor's new game—called "chess"—the Raja offers the inventor, Sissa, any reward he desires. Sissa asks the king for 1 grain of rice for the 1st square on the chess board, and then to double the number for every subsequent square (2 for the 2nd, 4 for the 3rd square. By the time they reach the 10th square, Sissa has 512 grains. This amount is doubled (1,024 grains) on the 11th square. By the 20th square, the number is over 500,000 grains. By the 64th square, the number is so high, the king cannot pay. We see a very similar tale of exponential growth in the modern telling by Demi: *One Grain of Rice* (New York: Scholastic Press, 1997). For a retelling of the Sissa story, see I. G. Edmonds, *Trickster Tales* (Philadelphia: J. P. Lippincott Co.,1966) pp. 5-13.

STOCKS AND FLOWS

An amount of something—trees, fish, people, goods, money—is a stock. The rate at which a stock changes, going up or down, is its flow. In a bathtub the accumulation of water in the tub is the stock; the faucet controls the inflow into the stock, and the drain at the bottom of the tub controls the outflow. Stocks and flows create many of the most perplexing dynamics we encounter, because stocks tend to accumulate. Studies of the pesticide DDT (dichlorodiphenyltrichloroethane), for example, have shown that while DDT evaporates from the surface of plants and buildings over six months, it remains in the tissue of fish for up to 50 years. The amount of DDT in fish tissue is a stock with very slow outflow. We need to understand these accumulations to understand the source of many of the major challenges we face today, both economic and environmental. When we understand stocks and flows, we understand that a deficit (the rate at which a country borrows money) is a flow and the national debt is a stock. We understand, as well, that taking the national deficit down to zero doesn't mean we get rid of the debt. We also understand that proposals to slow the rate of growth of carbon dioxide emissions will continue to increase the stock of carbon dioxide in our atmosphere, if the rate at which carbon dioxide flowing into the atmosphere continues to be greater than the rate at which it is draining out.

APPENDIX B

FINDING THE FOLKTALES

Finding modern wisdom in ancient stories is not new. Swiss psychologist and psychiatrist Carl Jung and American anthropologist Joseph Campbell both saw recurring themes or motifs in the world's myths and folklore. While Jung used these motifs to explain and explore the collective unconscious of humans, Campbell used myths to explain "the hero's journey," a motif common to peoples across the globe, regardless of culture or location. I now understand the thrill they must have felt when finding a similar motif in a folktale from Russia, India, Korea, or South America. When we read the world's folktales, we step into an ancient river, a continuous flow of insight and wisdom that was here thousands of years before and will be here for thousands of years to come.

I found many of the folktales for this book by following the motifs identified in *The Storyteller's Sourcebook: A Subject, Title, and Motif Index to Folklore Collections for Children* by Margaret Read MacDonald (Detroit: Gale, 1982) and Stith Thompson's *The Motif-Index of Folk-Literature* (Bloomington: Indiana University Press, 1966). It's easy to become overwhelmed by the sheer volume of folktale subjects and motifs. There are over 900 folktale subjects, such as animals, monsters, tests, deceptions, and pride.Within those subjects there are over 40,000 distinct motifs. These range from the well-known "rescue of princess/maiden from giant/monster" to the less familiar, for example "woman gives birth to a pumpkin." Since there are no subjects or motifs clearly marked "living systems," I looked for motifs that suggested characteristics of living systems, for instance, tightly coupled interrelationships, behavior, the importance of (bio)diversity and behavior that reinforces, diminishes, or oscillates over time. With the help of knowledgeable and helpful librarians, used-book-store owners, and the occasional Internet order, I was then able to track down most of the folktales I sought.

The story of *Gluskabe* in Chapter 9, for instance, can be linked to several motifs including "provisions for the future" and "one should not be too greedy." Greed is not a static thing; it tends to grow. Anything that grows in a folktale—greed, hunger, wealth, anger, happiness, or desire—indicates that the story can teach us about the dynamics of living systems because these systems also grow and change.

The folktale motif "chains of interdependent members" caught my eye because living systems are made up of tightly coupled, interdependent relationships. It led me to "Gecko's Complaint" (Chapter 1). The motif "What is most useful?" sounded familiar. When we ask that question of living systems, the answer is most often "No one part or process is more useful than another," and the tellers of the folktale "The Parts of the House Argue" (Chapter 2) agree.

Jung and Campbell used folktales and myths to help us understand the collectiveness of the human experience. I now understand, after my own extended journey into folktales, that this universality extends to our natural world as well.

FOLKTALE SOURCES

The folktales selected for this book have been adapted from original sources, whenever possible.

"Gecko's Complaint" is adapted from *Folk Tales from Bali and Lombok* retold by Margaret Muth Alibasah, (Jakarta: Djambatan, 1990), pp. 30-35. There are also two delightful picture books out now based on the same folktale (*Gecko's Complaint: A Balinese Folktale*, by Ann Martin Bowler [North Clarendon, VT: Charles E. Tuttle Publishing, 2003] and *Go to Sleep, Gecko!: A Balinese Folktale* by Margaret Reed MacDonald [Little Rock, AR: August House, 2006]).

I adapted "The Parts of the House Argue" from the original found in *Once in the First Times: Folktales from the Philippines,* by Elisabeth Hough Sechrist (Philadelphia: Macrae Smith Co., 1969). There is another wonderful version of this tale, particularly good for reading aloud, in Heather Forest's anthology *Wisdom Tales from Around the World* (Little Rock, AR: August House, 1996).

The tale "Kanu Above, Kanu Below" was originally told by the Limba people, who live in the Republic of Sierra Leone in West Africa.I adapted this telling from Margaret Read MacDonald's version in her book, *The Story Teller's Start-up Book* (Little Rock, AR: August House, 1993).

"Stone Soup," the story of a soup made out of a stone, has been told in many ways in many countries. A wanderer, typically a soldier or a tramp, convinces villagers to make a soup or stew out of a stone, a hatchet, or a nail. The Russian-Yiddish version can be found in *The Three Rolls and One Doughnut: Fables from Russia* by Mirra Ginsburg (New York: Dial, 1970). "Stone Stew," a version from England, can be found in I. G. Edmonds, *Trickster Tales*. I am also fond of the picture book *Stone Soup: An Old Tale*, retold and illustrated by Marcia Brown (New York: Simon & Schuster, 1947). I adapted the French version of "Stone Soup" from *The Soup Stone* by Maria Leach (New York: Funk & Wagnalls Co., 1954).

Nasreddin Hodja was a wise and witty philosopher and teacher. He was born in Turkey in around 1208 and became one of Turkey's best-known tricksters. I adapted "The Hodja's Tale of Pumpkin Vines and the Walnut Tree" from *Once the Hodja*, by Alice Geer Kelsey (New York: David McKay Co. Inc., 1943).

The tale "Too Much Sky" was adapted from "Why the Sky Is Far Away," a Bindi tale from Nigeria. It is found in the collection of folktales *In the*

92

Beginning ... Creation Stories for Young People, edited by Edward Lavitt and Robert E. McDowell (New York: Odarkai Books, The Third Press, 1973). Other versions of this story can be found in Ulli Beier's *The Origin of Life and Death: African Creation Myths* (London: Heinemann Educational Books, Ltd., 1966) and Margaret Read MacDonald's *Earth Care: World Folktales to Talk About* (North Haven, CT: Linnet Books, 1999).

I adapted "The Tale of the Sands" from a version found in *Tales of the Dervishes: Teaching-Stories of the Sufi Masters over the Past Thousand Years* by Idries Shah (New York: Arkana, 1993). Sufism is a mystical religion that developed from Islam, in the region that now includes Lebanon, Syria, Turkey, Iran, and Iraq. Sufi tales are have long been valued for their ability to open the mind and entertain.

"The Food of Paradise" was also adapted from *Tales of the Dervishes: Teaching-Stories of the Sufi Masters over the Past Thousand Years.*

"Gluskabe Traps the Animals," a North American Eastern Woodlands Native American folktale, is adapted from Joseph Bruchac's retelling in *Family of Earth and Sky: Indigenous Tales of Nature from around the World* by John Elder and Hertha D. Wong (Boston: Beacon Press, 1994. There is also a wonderful retelling of this tale in Heather Forest's *Wisdom Tales from Around the World* (Little Rock, AR: August House, 1996).

Aesop, once a Greek slave, lived in the 6th century BCE. He created more than 100 fables, most of which reveal the wise and foolish behavior of humankind. "Hercules and Pallas," a lesser-known fable by Aesop, was adapted from the version found in T*he Best Loved Fables of Aesop*, edited by Joseph Jacobs (New York: Gramercy Publishing, 2004).

This version of the Burmese folktale "A Kingdom Lost for a Drop of Honey" is adapted from *A Kingdom Lost for a Drop of Honey and other Burmese Folktales* by Maung Htin Aung and Helen G. Trager (New York: Parents' Magazine Press, 1968).

"The Rice Puller of Chaohwa" is adapted from a version in Harold Courlander's *The Tiger's Whisker and Other Tales from Asia and t   Pacific* (New York: Henry Holt, 1995). Courlander's version is ba translation by Hsin-Chih Lee and Cho-Feng L. Lee of a story reco.   , Chinese philosopher Mencius (Meng-tse), who lived during the 4th and 3rd centuries BCE.